Frightened Flier!

Nancy watched Todd reach into his backpack. He yanked out a glass jar filled with big fat beetles.

Oh, great, Nancy thought. Todd is holding the jar in front of Bess's face.

"Eeeeek!" Bess cried.

"Squaaaaaawk!" Carmen screeched.

The blue parrot hopped off Ranger Lynn's arm. She flapped her wings and flew out the door.

"Oh, no," Nancy groaned. "Carmen has flown the coop!"

The Nancy Drew Notebooks

Available from MINSTREL Books

THE
NANCY DREW
NOTEBOOKS®

#31

The Fine-Feathered Mystery

CAROLYN KEENE
ILLUSTRATED BY JAN NAIMO JONES

A
MINSTREL®
BOOK

Published by POCKET BOOKS
New York   London   Toronto   Sydney   Tokyo   Singapore

A MINSTREL PAPERBACK *Original*

A Minstrel Book published by
POCKET BOOKS, a division of Simon & Schuster Inc.
1230 Avenue of the Americas, New York, NY 10020

ISBN: 0-671-02785-9

First Minstrel Books printing June 1999

10 9 8 7 6 5 4 3 2 1

Cover art by Joanie Schwarz

Printed in the U.S.A.

QBP/✳

The Fine-Feathered Mystery

1

Birds of a Feather

Don't worry, Bess," eight-year-old Nancy Drew told her best friend. "We're going into the birdhouse, not the bughouse."

"Are you sure?" Bess Marvin asked nervously. She twisted a strand of her long blond hair around one finger.

Nancy's other best friend, George Fayne, rolled her dark eyes. "Give me a break, Bess," she told her cousin. "You're acting like you've never seen a bug before."

"I have," Bess said. "That's the problem!"

It was summer vacation, and the first day of Park Pals. For two weeks Nancy, Bess, and George would meet every day at the River Heights park. They would learn about birds, trees, and even bugs.

The girls had already met their leader, Ranger Lynn. They also met the other kids in their group, Joey Fusco, Andrea Singh, and Todd Steckler.

"Isn't the name of our group cool?" George asked. She began to hop on one foot. "The Grasshoppers."

Nancy nodded. "And the best part is, we're all in third grade."

Todd Steckler stepped in front of the girls. "I want to be a Bullfrog," he said.

"So?" George said with a shrug. "Jump up and down and croak."

"Du-uh!" Todd said. He pushed his glasses up the bridge of his nose. "I meant I want to be in the Bullfrog *group*."

"The Bullfrogs are for fifth graders," Nancy told Todd. "Aren't you in the third grade like us?"

"So what?" Todd said. "I know more about nature than anybody here. I'm going to be a park ranger some day."

Nancy giggled. Todd was already dressed like a park ranger. He wore a

2

dark green shirt and matching shorts. His ranger hat was just like Lynn's, and he carried a red backpack over one shoulder.

Bess grabbed Nancy's arm. She pointed to three plastic bug pins on Todd's shirt.

"Eew!" Bess cried. "They look real."

"I wish they were," Todd said. He patted his spider pin. "Bugs are excellent. Except for grasshoppers. They're dumb."

Nancy frowned. She knew Todd was talking about them.

"Why don't you be like your pins," George snapped, "and bug off?"

"Very funny," Todd snapped back. He turned around and walked over to Joey.

"I wish he *was* in the Bullfrogs," Bess said. "Then he wouldn't be in our group."

Ranger Lynn clapped her hands for attention.

"Are you all ready to visit the aviary?" Lynn asked. She pointed to a small brick building behind them.

"Aviary?" Andrea said. "I thought we were going into the birdhouse."

Todd sighed. "An aviary *is* a birdhouse. Bird brain."

3

"Todd is right," Lynn said. "An aviary is where we keep birds. But that was a very good question, Andrea."

Andrea stuck her tongue out at Todd. Then they followed Lynn into the aviary.

"Wow!" Nancy said.

There were three big cages filled with all kinds of colorful birds. They sat on perches and made loud, squawking sounds.

"Awesome," George gasped.

"They're so pretty," Bess said.

Nancy covered her ears and giggled. "And *noisy*," she said.

Lynn led the group to a tall cage. It was filled with brightly colored birds.

"Here are the tropical birds," she said. "Have any of you ever seen a parrot before?"

Nancy, Bess, and George looked at each other and smiled.

"Our friend Katie has a parrot named Lester," Nancy said. "She takes him everywhere she goes."

"So you girls probably know a lot about parrots," Lynn said.

4

"I know even more," Todd said. He stuck out his chin. "I know that parrots have pointy beaks so they can crack nuts. I know that parrots are the best climbers of all birds. I know that parrots can talk—"

"Not as much as *you* do," Joey interrupted.

Nancy and the Grasshoppers laughed.

"Very funny," Todd grumbled.

The group turned back to the cage. Nancy saw a big blue parrot sitting alone on a perch. It was the most beautiful bird she had ever seen.

"Bess, George, look!" Nancy said.

George gave a whistle. "I never saw a parrot that color before."

"It's almost violet," Bess said.

"That's Carmen," Lynn said. "She's a hyacinth macaw. A macaw is a kind of parrot."

"Isn't a hyacinth a flower?" Nancy asked.

"Yes," Lynn said. "Very good, Nancy."

"I knew that," Todd mumbled.

"Nancy," Bess whispered. "That parrot is the same color as something else."

5

"It is?" Nancy asked. "What?"

"Your detective notebook," Bess said.

"You're right, Bess," Nancy said.

Nancy's detective notebook *was* bright blue. She wrote her clues in it whenever she worked on a new mystery. She also carried it wherever she went.

"Shall we get a closer look at Carmen?" Lynn asked.

The Grasshoppers nodded as Lynn unlocked the cage and reached in.

"Arrk!" Carmen squawked as she jumped from the perch onto Lynn's arm.

"Where do hyacinth macaws come from?" Andrea asked.

"South America," Lynn said. "But there aren't many left. That's why they have to be protected."

"Are they endangered?" Nancy asked.

"Yes," Lynn said. "But as long as we keep Carmen here, she might have babies. Then there'll be more hyacinth macaws."

"Rrraaaaa!" Carmen squawked.

"Polly wanna cracker?" Joey joked.

"Parrots like crackers," Lynn said. "They also eat fruit, nuts, and small bugs."

"Bugs?" Bess shrieked. "That's the grossest thing I ever heard."

"Bugs are not gross," Todd insisted.

Nancy watched Todd reach into his backpack. He yanked out a glass jar filled with big fat beetles.

"These guys showed up when we turned on the porch lights," Todd said. "Are they neat or what?"

Oh, great, Nancy thought. Todd is holding the jar in front of Bess's face.

"Quit it, Todd!" Nancy scolded.

But it was too late. Bess let out the loudest scream that Nancy had ever heard.

"Eeeeek!" Bess cried.

"Squaaaaawk!" Carmen screeched.

The blue parrot hopped off Lynn's arm. She flapped her wings and flew toward the open door.

"Carmen!" Lynn called. She waved her arms in the air. "Come back!"

Everyone stared as Carmen flew out of the door and into the park.

"Oh, no," Nancy groaned. "Carmen has flown the coop!"

2

Creepy Crawlies

Let's go, Grasshoppers!" Lynn called. She waved her hand toward the door. "Maybe Carmen is right outside."

Nancy and the Grasshoppers followed Lynn out the door. They looked around.

"Carmen!" Nancy called.

"Come out, come out, wherever you are!" George called.

But Carmen was gone.

Todd pointed his finger at Bess. "It's all her fault. She screamed and scared Carmen away."

Nancy looked at Bess. Bess looked as if she was about to cry.

"Bess wouldn't have screamed if you

9

hadn't put those bugs right in her face," Nancy told Todd.

"Yeah," George said. "You and your stupid bugs."

Todd hugged the jar to his chest. "They're not stupid," he said.

Just then Nancy saw a tall man in a ranger's uniform walking toward them.

"Who's that?" Nancy asked.

"That's Ranger Roy, the head ranger at the park," Todd said. "He's my hero!"

"Good morning, Grasshoppers," Ranger Roy said.

Todd gave a little salute. "Good morning, Ranger Roy, sir!" he barked.

"Oh, brother," George mumbled.

"And what did you all do this morning, Grasshoppers?" Ranger Roy asked.

The Grasshoppers looked at one another nervously. But Todd saluted again.

"We lost an endangered bird—sir!" he snapped.

"An endangered bird?" Ranger Roy said. He looked at Lynn. "Is this true?"

10

Lynn nodded sadly. "Carmen got frightened and flew out of the aviary."

"Carmen is our hyacinth macaw," Ranger Roy said. "This is serious. Very serious."

Todd leaned over to Bess. "And it's all your fault!" he whispered.

Ranger Roy called an emergency meeting in the main house. All of the Park Pals were there.

"Butterflies, Caterpillars, Grasshoppers, Sparrows, Bullfrogs," Ranger Roy said. "We have a big problem."

Nancy and her friends sat on the floor with the other groups. They watched Ranger Roy pace back and forth.

"Carmen the parrot is missing," Ranger Roy said. He held up a picture of a hyacinth macaw. "She's bright blue, weighs three pounds, and is three feet long."

Todd jumped up. "A hyacinth macaw is the biggest kind of parrot there is!"

"Thank you, Todd," Ranger Roy said.

Todd smiled and sat back down. A Butterfly girl raised her hand.

"My cat always comes home when she's hungry," she said. "Maybe Carmen will, too."

Todd jumped up again.

"No way," he said. "There are plenty of berries and bugs all over River Heights. She can pig out."

Nancy tried to ignore Todd. She raised her hand.

"Yes?" Ranger Roy asked.

"Maybe Carmen will come back if she misses her friends," Nancy suggested.

Todd let out a big sigh. "Hel-lo? Carmen can always make new friends. Birds of a feather flock together, you know."

George grabbed Todd's arm and pulled him down. "Sit down, will you?"

Ranger Rick looked at the kids seriously. "I'm going to spread the word about Carmen right away. But I want the search to begin right here."

"Here?" a Bullfrog boy asked. "You want us to look for Carmen?"

"You bet," Ranger Roy said. "And this might help."

12

Nancy and her friends watched Ranger Roy pop a cassette into a tape recorder. He pressed a button. Soon the sound of a parrot's singing voice filled the room:

"I'm a happy camper!
That's what I like to do!
Why don't you come and join me?
And be a camper too?
La, la, laaaa!"

Ranger Roy clicked off the tape recorder and sighed.

"That was Carmen singing her favorite song," he said. "Learn it. Remember it. And listen for it wherever you go."

The room was silent until Bess raised her hand.

"How do we catch Carmen?" she asked.

"The best way to catch a bird is to lead a trail of bird seed into a cage," Ranger Roy said. "I'll gather some ingredients today. We'll whip up a batch of my special seed salad tomorrow."

Todd jumped up. "Will there be a prize

13

for the kid who finds Carmen?" he asked.

Ranger Roy nodded. "The person who finds Carmen will be made an official Junior Park Ranger."

Todd's eyes lit up. "You mean with a uniform? And a badge?"

"You betcha," Ranger Roy said.

Todd pumped his fist in the air. "Ye-es! A park ranger—at last!"

"What a pest," Bess whispered.

"I wish *he* were endangered," George hissed.

"So good luck, Park Pals," Ranger Roy said. "And let's bring our bird home."

The kids gave each other high-fives. Then they stood up to leave.

"It would be fun being a park ranger just like Lynn," Nancy said.

"Well, forget it," Todd said meanly. "You girls don't have a chance."

"What do you mean?" Bess asked.

"I'm going to find Carmen," Todd said. "Even if I have to climb every tree in River Heights."

Bess planted her hands on her hips.

"George is the best tree climber in River Heights," she said. "But if anyone is going to find Carmen, it's Nancy."

"Nancy?" Todd asked.

"Me?" Nancy asked.

"Nancy is a great detective," Bess said proudly. "She even carries a blue detective notebook in her pocket."

"Oh, yeah?" Todd said. He pointed to Nancy's pants pocket. "Let me see it."

Nancy grabbed her pocket. "No way!"

"Well, so what?" Todd sneered. "I'm still going to find Carmen. And when I do I'll be an official Junior Park Ranger."

The girls watched as Todd smiled slowly. "Hey . . . maybe they'll even name a bug after me," he said.

"They already have," George snapped. "The worm."

Todd frowned. "That was so funny I forgot to laugh."

"It doesn't matter who finds Carmen," Nancy said. "The most important thing is to bring her home."

"Nancy's right," Bess said. She turned to her friends. "Let's go."

Todd flashed a wicked smile. "See ya."

Nancy, Bess, and George turned away from Todd. They began to walk toward Lynn and the other Grasshoppers.

"Todd thinks he knows everything about birds and bugs," Bess said.

"Well, he's starting to bug *me!*" George said.

The girls giggled. Suddenly George stopped walking.

"Um . . . Nancy?" she asked slowly.

"What is it, George?" Nancy asked.

"Speaking of bugs," George said. "What's that thing on your shoulder?"

"Thing?" Nancy gulped.

She looked down and screamed. Crawling up her shoulder was a fat black beetle.

"Yuck!" Nancy cried. She jumped up and down until the bug dropped to the floor.

Nancy was still shaking when she looked up. She saw Todd laughing and shaking his bug jar.

"You should have seen your face," Todd laughed. "And you didn't even know I put it on your shoulder! Ha! Ha!"

Nancy turned to her friends.

"Remember what I said about not caring who finds Carmen?" she asked.

George and Bess nodded.

"Well, I've changed my mind," Nancy said. She folded her hands across her chest. "This means war!"

3

Follow That Bird!

How are you going to find Carmen, Nancy?" Bess asked later that afternoon.

The girls were having milk and cookies in the Drews' kitchen.

"I'm going to solve this the way I solve any other mystery," Nancy said.

She opened her blue detective notebook on the table. On a fresh page she wrote, "Where's Carmen?"

"Okay," Nancy said. She twirled her pencil in her hand. "What are some important things we know about Carmen?"

Bess took a bite of a cookie. "She's a parrot."

George gave Bess a smirk. "She's a bright blue hyacinth macaw," she said.

Nancy bit into a cookie and studied the page. "We know that Carmen likes to sing the happy camper song."

"And her voice is a lot higher than Lester's," George said.

"Yeah," Bess said. "Lester goes *squawk,* and Carmen goes *arrrk!*"

George shook her head. "It's more like a *krraaaak!*"

"Isn't it more of a *rrrraaaah?*" Nancy asked with a giggle.

The girls began to laugh and make parrot sounds. The Drews' housekeeper, Hannah Gruen, walked into the kitchen.

"It sounds like a pet store in here," Hannah said, covering her ears.

"It's my new mystery, Hannah," Nancy said. "We're looking for a missing parrot."

"Did you say 'parrot'?" Hannah asked. Her eyes lit up. "As in . . . bird?"

"Yes," Nancy said. "Why?"

Hannah reached for something on the counter. It was a bright yellow T-shirt.

20

"Ta-daaaa!" she said, holding it up.

Nancy looked at the T-shirt. It said, River Heights Bird's-eye Brigade.

"I've joined a bird-watching club," Hannah explained. "We meet every Tuesday morning on Hazel Hill."

"What kind of birds do you see?" Bess asked.

"All kinds," Hannah said. "Our leader, Walt Whipperwill, says, if there's a special bird in River Heights, we'll see it."

Just then Nancy had an idea.

"Bess, George," she said. "Maybe the Bird's-eye Brigade will spot Carmen!"

"Who's Carmen?" Hannah asked.

"The parrot we're looking for," Nancy explained. "Tomorrow's Tuesday, Hannah. Can we bird-watch with you?"

"I don't see why not," Hannah said. "But we start very early in the morning."

"How early?" George asked. She took a sip of her milk.

"Five-thirty in the morning," Hannah said cheerfully.

George sputtered the milk she was drinking. "Five-thirty?"

Bess groaned. "I can't even wake up for school. And that's at seven-thirty."

"Oh, it'll be worth it," Hannah said. "Just last week I spotted a yellow-bellied sapsucker up in a chestnut tree."

"How did you know it was there?" Nancy asked.

Hannah winked. "A little birdy told me," she said.

That night after dinner, Nancy told her dad all about the missing parrot. Carson Drew was a lawyer and often helped Nancy with her cases.

"Going on the bird-watch is a good idea, Pudding Pie," Mr. Drew said.

"It is?" Nancy asked excitedly.

Mr. Drew picked up his newspaper and nodded. "You should find out if Carmen is still in River Heights."

"What if she isn't, Daddy?" Nancy asked, worried.

"Then I guess this case will be for the birds," Mr. Drew teased.

"Oh, Daddy," Nancy groaned. "Not another bird joke—please!"

It was still dark when Nancy woke up the next morning. It was even dark when she climbed into Hannah's car.

Hannah was dressed for a morning of bird-watching. She wore a hat, backpack, and rubber boots, and carried huge binoculars.

On the way to Hazel Hill they picked up Bess and George. They both looked very sleepy.

"I was so tired I poured orange juice on my corn flakes," Bess groaned.

George yawned. "I almost brushed my teeth with ointment."

"I'm not sleepy at all," Nancy said.

"Well, rise and shine," Hannah said as she drove. "Because here's Hazel Hill."

It was just getting light as Nancy and her friends stepped out of the car.

Five other people dressed like Hannah were standing under a tree. A man with tan shorts and a matching vest waved them over.

"Morning, Hannah," he called.

"Girls," Hannah said. "I'd like you to meet our eagle-eyed leader, Walt Whipperwill."

"Hi," Nancy said. "These are my friends Bess and George. They're a little sleepy this morning."

"Sleepy?" Walt chuckled. "Don't you know that the early bird catches the worm?"

The other bird-watchers laughed.

Walt leaned over and winked. "Except for the owls . . . they don't give a hoot!"

The bird-watchers laughed even louder.

"It's too early for bird jokes," George whispered to Nancy.

"Are you girls looking for a special bird this morning?" Walt asked.

"Yes," Nancy said. "A hyacinth macaw."

"A hyacinth macaw?" Walt asked. He gave a whistle. "That's a serious bird."

"I know," Nancy said. "And we're serious about finding her."

"Okay, brigade," Walt said. He turned to the other birdwatchers. "Let's spread out and keep our eyes peeled. If we're lucky, we'll see some warblers."

The brigade chattered excitedly.

"Where should my friends and I go, Mr. Whipperwill?" Nancy asked.

Walt pointed to a bench under a tree. "Why don't you girls *perch* yourselves right over there?" he suggested.

Nancy, Bess, and George sat on the bench. They stared up at the trees.

"These should help," George said. She pulled a pair of plastic binoculars from her backpack.

"Way to go, George!" Nancy said. She looked through the binoculars. It made the branches seem very close.

Bess yawned. "What do you see, Nancy?"

"Some sparrows, a squirrel," Nancy said. "But no hyacinth macaw."

Nancy sighed and lowered the binoculars. She turned to Bess and George. They

were curled up on the bench—and fast asleep!

"Bess, George," Nancy hissed. She shook her friends gently. "Wake up."

Bess mumbled something and rolled over. George was already snoring.

Oh, great, Nancy thought. How can they fall asleep at a time like this?

Nancy listened to George snore. She watched Bess sleeping.

"I'm not tired at all," Nancy thought. She gave a little yawn. "Not really."

But then Nancy's eyelids became heavy. She felt herself getting sleepier and sleepier.

"I won't fall asleep," Nancy said to herself. She yawned. "No . . . way."

The next thing Nancy knew, Hannah was shaking her arm.

"Nancy! Nancy!"

Nancy opened her eyes. "Wha-what?" she asked.

"You fell asleep," Hannah said.

"Sleep?" Nancy blinked her eyes. "I couldn't have."

Bess and George sat up. They rubbed their eyes.

"What happened?" George asked.

"Did we miss something?" Bess asked.

"You sure did," Hannah said. "We just spotted a hyacinth macaw."

Nancy gave a little shriek.

"Did you say 'a hyacinth macaw'?"

4

Deep Blue Clue

Why didn't you wake us up, Nancy?" Bess complained.

Nancy didn't answer Bess. She jumped up from the bench and ran to the other bird-watchers. They were staring up at a tree through big binoculars.

"She's a beauty, all right," Walt said, looking through his binoculars.

Nancy saw a flash of bright blue in the tree. Then she heard a squawk.

"Bess, George," Nancy cried. "Listen!"

The girls strained their ears.

"I'm a happy camper," a voice squawked. "That's what I like to dooooo!"

"Nancy!" Bess said. She jumped up and down. "It's the happy camper song!"

"It's Carmen!" Nancy cried. She tugged at Walt's sleeve. "Mr. Whipperwill, Mr. Whipperwill, you have to catch that bird."

"Catch it?" Walt asked. "Now, why would we want to do that?"

Nancy stared at Walt. "Because we have to bring her back to the park."

Walt shook his head and laughed. "We're *bird-watchers*. Not bird-catchers."

"Now you tell us," George groaned.

Nancy heard the leaves rustle. Then she saw Carmen stick her head out.

"Rrrraaak!" she squawked. "Happy camper. Happy camper."

"There she is," Nancy cried. She raised her arm. "Come here, Carmen!"

Carmen swooped down from the tree. But instead of landing on Nancy's arm, she flew away and out of sight.

"Oh, nooooo!" Nancy cried.

"There she goes," Walt said. He turned to the other bird-watchers. "Did everyone see that excellent hyacinth macaw?"

The bird-watchers nodded excitedly. But George was angry.

"We saw her, all right," George said. "We saw her fly away."

Nancy put her hand on George's shoulder. "It's okay, George. It's still a good thing we saw Carmen."

"How come?" Bess asked.

"Because now we know that Carmen is still here in River Heights," Nancy said.

"And not South America," Bess said.

Nancy took out a pencil and wrote the clue in her notebook.

When they were finished bird-watching, Hannah drove the girls to Park Pals. They met Lynn and the other Grasshoppers inside their brick clubhouse.

"Don't tell the others about our Carmen sighting," Nancy whispered to Bess and George. "We don't want Todd to know."

The girls sat down at a long table with the other Grasshoppers.

"What are we doing today?" Nancy asked.

"We're making bird seed salad," Andrea said. "To attract Carmen."

Joey nodded from across the table. "It's Ranger Roy's special recipe."

Ranger Roy joined Lynn at the front of the room. He wore an apron that read, This Food Is for the Birds!

"Okay, Grasshoppers," Ranger Roy said. "Lynn will pass out the ingredients. Then we're going to mix them up real good."

Lynn passed out small bowls of nuts, seeds, dried berries, and corn. She also gave the Grasshoppers mixing bowls and spoons.

"Carmen will love this," Lynn said. "It has everything she likes to eat."

"Not *everything*," Todd said.

"What's missing?" Ranger Roy asked.

Todd reached into his pocket and pulled out a small cricket. "Bugs!" he said. "Lots and lots of crunchy bugs!"

Bess jumped up. She was about to scream when Ranger Roy held up his hand.

"Todd Steckler," he said. "This is my recipe, and it does not call for bugs."

Todd sighed. "Sorry, Ranger Roy."

The cricket chirped as Todd tossed him out of an open window.

"Thank goodness," Bess whispered.

"Now," Ranger Roy said. He rubbed his hands together. "Let's get cookin'."

Nancy and the Grasshoppers mixed the ingredients well. Then they carefully poured the mix into small plastic bags.

"Remember," Ranger Roy said when they were done. "Sprinkle a trail of seeds into a cage. It's the best way to catch a bird."

"But not the *only* way," Todd whispered.

"What do you mean?" Nancy asked.

Todd winked over his glasses. "I've come up with some brilliant plans to catch Carmen."

"Like what?" Bess asked.

"Do you think I'm stupid?" Todd snapped. "I'm not telling *you*."

Then he stood up and walked over to Ranger Roy.

"What do you think he's going to do?" Bess asked.

"He's probably going to build some kind of trap," Nancy said.

"We can build a trap, too!" George said excitedly.

"Yeah!" Bess said. She tilted her head. "How?"

"We already have the seed salad," Nancy said. "But birdcages are expensive."

"Maybe we can borrow one from Katie," Bess suggested.

"Katie and her family might still be on their trip," Nancy said.

"We don't *need* a cage," George said. "We can buy a big butterfly net at the Bow-Wow Shop on Main Street."

"Good idea, George," Nancy said.

"Our trap will be the best ever," Bess said. "We'll show that Todd Steckler."

After Park Pals was over for the day, Mrs. Marvin picked the girls up in her red minivan.

While she shopped on Main Street, the girls went to the Bow-Wow Shop. George bought a butterfly net, and Nancy bought a plastic bird feeder.

"Now that we have our trap supplies," Nancy said, "we'd better plan our trap."

"Relax, Nancy," George said. "I'm sure we're way ahead of everyone else."

Bess shook her head. She pointed down Main Street. "I don't think so," she said.

Nancy gasped. Main Street was filled with Park Pals looking for Carmen.

Andrea was taping drawings of Carmen to lampposts. Joey was dressed in a bird costume he'd worn for Halloween. He was handing out flyers that read Parrot Missing!

A Caterpillar boy was tooting a bird caller. Two Bullfrog girls were singing the happy camper song.

"Oh, no," George cried. "River Heights has gone parrot crazy!"

Nancy sighed. "I guess everyone wants to be a Junior Park Ranger."

The girls walked down Main Street to meet Mrs. Marvin. Suddenly Nancy saw something that made her stop.

"What is it, Nancy?" Bess asked.

Nancy pointed to a store in the middle of the block. A sign on the window said, The Beak of Perfection.

"That's a fancy store that sells parrots," Nancy said.

"Isn't that where the Zaleskis bought Lester?" George asked.

"Yes," Nancy said. "He was a birthday present for Katie."

Nancy, Bess, and George peeked inside the window. They could see all kinds of birds sitting on perches.

"Ohmygosh," Nancy gasped. She pressed her face against the window. "There's a deep blue parrot in there!"

Bess and George pressed their faces against the glass.

"I see it!" Bess squealed. "It's the same color as Carmen."

Nancy looked away from the window at her friends. "But *is* it Carmen?"

5

A Perfect Trap

We have to go inside to check out that bird," George said.

Nancy nodded. She took out her notebook and wrote down the clue.

"If it is Carmen," Bess asked, "why would she end up in a store?"

"Hyacinth macaws must be very valuable," Nancy said. "The store owner might have caught Carmen. And now he's selling her for lots of money."

"I guess we'll have to go inside, huh, Nancy?" Bess asked excitedly.

Nancy nodded. She slipped her notebook back into her pocket.

The three friends were about to go

inside when a man with a mustache stepped in front of them. The name tag on his jacket read, Robert Salazar.

"Can I help you?" Mr. Salazar asked.

"We'd like to see some of your birds," Nancy said politely.

George hid the butterfly net behind her back. "Your blue birds."

"Sorry," Mr. Salazar said. "But children are not allowed in the store."

"We just want to look," Bess said.

Mr. Salazar stared down his nose at the girls. "That's the problem," he said. "The store is for serious customers only."

A phone rang in the back of the store. Mr. Salazar turned around and walked away. He slipped behind a red curtain. "He's not Mr. Robert Salazar," Bess snapped. "He's Snobby Bobby."

"And who says we're not serious?" George complained. "We're serious— about finding Carmen."

Nancy stuck her head inside the door. "He's somewhere in the back," she whispered. "Let's take a quick look around."

The girls tiptoed into the store. Nancy glanced at the birds. They were all colors—red, green, and yellow.

"Wow," George said. "Snobby Bobby has some awesome birds."

"Shh," Nancy warned. She walked over to the blue parrot. But the parrot wasn't totally blue. It had a bright yellow chest.

"Phooey," Nancy said. "It's not Carmen."

She turned around to leave. Suddenly she saw something that made her jaw drop. Bess was feeding seed salad to a bright red-and-green parrot.

"Bess," Nancy hissed. "Don't feed the birds!"

Bess jumped. The bag of seed salad flew out of her hand and into the air. Then it dropped to the floor with a *splat!*

"Oh, no!" Nancy said. She watched the seeds spill all over the floor.

The birds began to squawk and screech. They swooped down from their perches toward the seed salad.

"Shoo! Shoo!" George said. She waved her butterfly net over the birds.

40

Nancy and Bess tried to sweep up the seeds but it was no use. The parrots were digging in and talking up a storm.

"*Arrrk!* Chow time!"

"*Rrrraaaaak!* Come and get it!"

Nancy's heart pounded. The parrots were eating and kicking seeds all over the store. They were in big trouble now!

Mr. Salazar ran out from the back.

"What is the meaning of this?" he cried. "And why are you feeding my birds?"

The red-and-green parrot flapped its wings and began to squawk.

"Snobby Bobby! Snobby Bobby! *Krrrakkk!*"

Mr. Salazar stared at the girls. "What did he just say?"

"Um," George said. She rested the butterfly net on her shoulder. "We were just . . . leaving."

The girls dashed out of the store and into Mrs. Marvin's van. They plopped down in the backseat, out of breath.

"Why did you have to feed the birds,

Bess?" George asked as the car drove away from Main Street.

"I was only feeding *one* bird," Bess said. "The rest was an accident."

Nancy stared out of the window. Finding Carmen was not going to be easy.

Mrs. Marvin guided the van around a corner. She drove up Katie Zaleski's block.

"Hey, look," Nancy said. She pointed out the window. "The Zaleskis are back from their trip. Their car is in the driveway."

"It looks as though they're getting a delivery," Mrs. Marvin said as she drove.

The girls looked out of the car window. A Crispy Cracker truck was parked in front of Katie's house. Two men were carrying big cardboard boxes toward the front door.

"All those crackers must be for Lester," Bess said. "He loves crackers."

"Hmm," Nancy said slowly. "Lester eats a lot of crackers. But not that many."

"Maybe the trip gave him a huge appetite," George said.

43

"I guess," Nancy said. But she still thought the big delivery was weird.

Mrs. Marvin dropped Nancy off at her house. It was close to dinnertime so the girls said goodbye.

"Let's meet at the park tomorrow an hour before Park Pals," Nancy said as she stepped out of the van. "That will give us time to set up our trap."

"What kind of a trap are we going to build?" George asked.

Nancy shrugged. "Who knows? But I have all night to think of one."

That night after dinner, Nancy sat on her bed. She glanced through her detective notebook. Her Labrador puppy, Chocolate Chip, was busy sniffing through her room.

"'Carmen is a hyacinth macaw. She has bright blue feathers. She's from South America,'" Nancy read out loud.

"*Woof!*" Chip barked.

"South America," Nancy repeated. She smiled down at her dog. "Chip, I think I have a super idea."

Nancy and Chip ran down the stairs and into the living room. Mr. Drew was sitting in his favorite chair, watching TV.

"Daddy?" Nancy asked. She walked over to her dad's music collection. "Do you have any South American music?"

"There's a CD with samba music," Mr. Drew said. "That's a dance they do in Brazil."

Nancy ran her finger along a stack of CDs until she found one called "Samba Saturday Night."

"Perfect!" she said. "Carmen's from South America. When she hears this music, she'll fly right over."

Mr. Drew chuckled. "Good thinking, Pudding Pie," he said.

"Thanks, Daddy," Nancy said. Chip jumped as she waved the CD in the air. "And I'll bet creepy Todd didn't think of this."

Just then Nancy saw something on the TV. A news reporter was standing in front of the park's aviary.

"Daddy," Nancy said, "make the TV louder, please."

Mr. Drew turned up the volume. Nancy listened as the reporter spoke into her microphone.

"Carmen, the hyacinth macaw, disappeared from the park yesterday morning," she said. "And we have an eyewitness right here."

Nancy's own eyes popped wide open. The eyewitness was Todd Steckler!

"I saw the whole thing," Todd told the reporter. "This girl named Bess screamed. Then Carmen flew away."

"Are you saying that Bess *scared* Carmen away?" the reporter asked.

"It was her fault all right," Todd said. He looked into the camera. "But don't worry, folks. I'm going to find Carmen."

Nancy folded her arms. She frowned at the TV set.

"Oh, yeah?" she said. "We'll just see about that, Todd Steckler!"

6

Treetop Terror

Did you hear what Todd said about me on the news last night?" Bess asked the next morning. "I felt like I was on that TV show—*America's Most Hunted!*"

"Forget about it, Bess," Nancy said. "Let's concentrate on our trap."

It was Wednesday morning. Mr. Fayne had dropped the girls off at the park an hour before Park Pals.

Nancy had brought her bird feeder, the samba music, and a portable CD player. George had brought her butterfly net and a bag of seed salad. Bess was so upset, she hadn't brought anything.

"Okay," Nancy said. "Where should we put down our trap?"

She felt George grab her arm.

"Nancy, check it out," George said, keeping her voice low. She pointed to a row of hedges.

Nancy gasped. A deep blue feather was sticking up behind the hedge.

"That feather is the same color as Carmen's," Nancy said.

George raised her butterfly net above her head. "Then it must be Carmen."

The blue feather bobbed up and down.

"Wait, George," Nancy whispered. "We have to get a closer look."

"What else could it be, Nancy?" George asked. She raised the net high. Then she tiptoed toward the feather.

The feather swayed back and forth as George stopped at the hedge.

"George," Nancy whispered. "Wait!"

George swung the net down over the feather. "Gotcha!" she shouted.

Nancy listened for a squawk. But instead she heard a loud scream.

An angry woman jumped up from behind the hedge. The net was over her head—and her blue-feathered hat!

"Uh-oh," Nancy groaned.

The woman pulled the net off her head. Then she pointed over the hedge.

"All I was doing was sitting and reading a newspaper on that bench," she said angrily. "When—wham!"

"I'm sorry," George said. She took back the net. "We thought you were Carmen."

The woman straightened her hat. She was wearing a bright blue sundress that matched the feather.

"Who on earth is Carmen?" she asked.

"A parrot," Bess said with a smile.

"You thought I was a parrot?" the woman gasped. "Well!"

The girls watched as the woman in the blue-feathered hat huffed off.

"You were right, Nancy." George sighed. "I should have gotten a closer look."

Nancy began to giggle. "That's okay, George. It *was* a funny hat."

The girls walked on through the park.

They stopped under a thick shade tree.

"This looks like a great place to set up our trap," Nancy said.

"All systems go," George said. She sprinkled seed salad around the tree.

Nancy set the CD player on the ground.

"What does music from Brazil sound like?" Bess asked.

"I don't know," Nancy said. She popped the CD into the player. "Let's listen."

Nancy pressed the Play button. The girls waited until they heard the first tune.

"Hey," George said. She snapped her fingers to the beat. "I like it."

Nancy liked the music, too. It was fast and had lots of drums.

"I feel like dancing," Bess said. She raised her hands over her head and twirled like a ballerina.

"Me, too!" Nancy said. She began to wiggle her hips. "Come on, George!"

"I'm not a great dancer," George said. But soon she was kicking her leg back and forth.

"What dance is *that?*" Bess asked.

"It's called the Soccer Samba!" George laughed.

The three friends giggled and danced to the music. But suddenly Nancy heard something else.

"Listen," Nancy said. She quickly turned off the music.

"What is it?" Bess asked.

Nancy pointed up. A squawking sound came from the tree.

"Arrrrk!"

"It sounds just like Carmen," Bess said. She jumped up and down excitedly.

"Arrrrk!"

"There it is again," Nancy said.

"I'm going up there," George insisted. She began to climb the tree.

"Arrrrk!"

"Wait for me!" Nancy called.

Bess held up the butterfly net. "You forgot this."

Nancy and George climbed halfway up the tree. The leaves began to rustle.

"Carmen?" Nancy called. "Is that you?"

The leaves parted. Sitting on a branch was a strange and ugly creature. It was covered with leaves and mud.

"Eeeeek!" Nancy and George both screamed as they clutched the tree.

"Is it a bird?" Bess called up.

"No!" Nancy cried. She and George jumped down from the tree. "It's some kind of shrub monster!"

7

Katie's Secret

The three friends shrieked as the shrub monster jumped down from the tree.

"Back!" George shouted. She swung her butterfly net. "You . . . you walking nest!"

Just then Nancy noticed something strange. The shrub monster was wearing big round glasses. Just like . . .

"Todd Steckler!" Nancy declared.

Todd brushed a clump of mud from his glasses. "You were expecting Godzilla?"

"Yuck!" Bess said. "Does your mom know you were playing in mud?"

Todd stuck out his leafy chin.

"It's called camouflage," he said. "I

didn't want Carmen to see me while I waited for her in the tree."

"Then where was that parrot noise coming from?" Nancy asked.

"This," Todd said. He raised a silver birdcall to his lips. Then he blasted it in Nancy's face.

"Arrrrrk!"

"Oww!" Nancy cried.

Todd laughed. He picked a twig from his hair. "When it comes to finding Carmen, I mean business."

"Well, so do we," George declared.

"Yeah," Bess said. She pointed to the trap. "We have a butterfly net, bird seed, and South American music."

"South American music?" Todd laughed. He looked at Nancy. "Is that the best you can do, Detective Drew?"

"What do you mean?" Nancy asked.

"You're a detective," Todd scoffed. "Why don't you use dogs to sniff for Carmen? Like they do on that TV show *America's Most Hunted.*"

Todd blasted his birdcall one more

time. Then he snickered and scurried back up the tree.

"I don't know what's worse," George muttered. "Finding a freak or a geek."

"Wait a minute," Nancy said. "Todd is right."

Bess made a face. "Todd?"

"Chocolate Chip is always sniffing around," Nancy said. "If she sniffs a parrot feather, she might be able to track Carmen down."

"Where are we going to get a parrot feather, Nancy?" Bess asked.

"From Katie," Nancy said. "She might have one of Lester's feathers lying around the house."

George glanced at her watch. "We can't go now. Park Pals is starting soon."

"We'll go *after* Park Pals," Nancy explained. "I'll go home and get permission to walk Chip to Katie's house."

"And I'll get permission to meet you there," George said.

"Me, too," Bess said. "This is such a cool idea, Nancy."

Nancy frowned at the tree. "Even if it is Todd Steckler's!"

The girls learned all about trees at Park Pals that morning. Todd couldn't join the group until he'd washed off all the mud and leaves.

When Park Pals was over, Nancy hurried home. She ate one of Hannah's tuna fish sandwiches. Then she walked Chip to Katie's house. Bess and George were waiting for her on Katie's block.

"Chip was sniffing all the way here," Nancy said proudly.

"Atta girl, Chip!" George said.

Nancy rang the Zaleskis' doorbell. Katie opened the door with Lester on her shoulder.

"Hi," Katie said.

"Hi! Hi!" Lester squawked. *"Raaak!"* Chip barked softly when she saw the parrot. Lester ruffled his feathers.

"How was your trip, Katie?" Nancy asked.

"Fun!" Katie said. "We visited Parrot Jungle in Florida. Lester loved it."

Lester blinked and rolled his head.

"How's Park Pals?" Katie asked.

"Great," George said. "We're looking for an endangered bird. She flew out of the aviary on Monday."

Katie's eyes opened wide. "What kind of bird?" she asked.

"A hyacinth macaw," Nancy said.

Katie's mouth dropped open. She closed it and gulped. "A hyacinth . . . macaw?"

Bess nodded. "Her name is Carmen. Did you hear about her, Katie?"

Katie shook her head so fast she hit Lester with her brown ponytail.

"No way," she said. "We just got back from Florida yesterday. How could we know?"

"Whoever finds Carmen will be made a Junior Park Ranger," Bess explained. "Is that cool or what?"

Katie stared down at her sneakers. "Way cool," she mumbled.

"Way cool!" Lester squawked.

"That's why we want one of Lester's

feathers," Nancy said. "So Chip can sniff it and find Carmen."

Katie's eyes opened wide. "A feather? You mean you want me to pluck him?"

"*Arrrk!*" Lester screeched. He ruffled up and flapped his wings.

"No! No!" Nancy said. "We just—"

Suddenly Lester opened his beak. Then he began to sing: "I'm a happy camper. That's what I like to doooooo."

The girls froze like statues.

"What did he just sing?" George asked.

"Who knows?" Katie said. She looked more nervous. "Probably some stupid song from the TV."

"That's Carmen's song!" Bess said.

"If Lester repeats everything he hears," Nancy said slowly, "then how did he hear Carmen?"

Just then Nancy remembered the boxes of crackers being loaded into the house.

"Katie?" Nancy asked. "Did you get a new parrot in the last few days?"

Katie shook her head. "A new parrot? Why would I want another parrot?"

Just then Nancy heard a squawk. But this time it didn't come from Lester. It came from inside the house.

"Phooey," Katie mumbled.

"You do have another parrot, Katie!" Nancy said. She tried to peek over Katie's shoulder.

"Is it a hyacinth macaw?" Bess asked excitedly.

"Is it Carmen?" George asked.

8

Home Tweet Home

Bess let out a little shriek. "Do you really have Carmen, Katie?" she asked.

Katie nodded. "When we came home from our trip she was sitting on my windowsill. She was so pretty that I brought her inside and put her in one of Lester's cages."

"Hmmm," Nancy said. "So that's the reason for all those crackers."

"What did your parents say when you found Carmen?" Nancy asked.

"They didn't know that Carmen was missing or endangered," Katie said. "So they said it was okay."

"Why did you want another parrot?" George asked.

"Lester was so happy around those other birds at Parrot Jungle," Katie said. "I saw how much he needed a friend."

"He'll make new friends," Bess said with a smile. "Birds of a feather flock together, you know."

"And the park will be so happy to get Carmen back," Nancy said.

"Back?" Katie asked. She planted her hands on her hips. "Who says I'm giving her back?"

Nancy stared at Katie.

"Katie, you have to give Carmen back," she said. "She belongs to the River Heights park. That's where she's protected."

"We can take her back there right now," George offered.

"No way!" Katie said. She spread her arms across the door. "You are not taking away Lester's friend."

"*Rrrraaaa!*" Lester screeched.

"But, Katie—" Nancy started to say.

"You'll do anything to become a silly Junior Park Ranger, Nancy," Katie said.

Nancy shook her head. "It's not that."

"Yes, it is," Katie said. Her eyes began to fill with tears. "Isn't it enough that you're a detective?"

The girls stared in silence as Katie went inside and closed the door.

"Should we tell Ranger Roy?" George finally asked.

Nancy shook her head. "We can't do that. Katie is our friend."

"What do we do, Nancy?" Bess asked.

"I don't know," Nancy said. She petted Chip sadly. "I just don't know."

That night Mr. Drew barbecued hamburgers in the backyard. But Nancy wasn't very hungry. She sat at the picnic table and told her dad all about Katie.

"If I tell Ranger Roy, then Katie might get in trouble," Nancy said.

Mr. Drew put a well-done hamburger on Nancy's plate. "Why don't you give Katie a chance to come forward herself?" he asked.

"But what if she never comes forward?" Nancy said. "What if she decides to keep Carmen forever and ever?"

"Then you have a big decision to make, Pudding Pie," Mr. Drew said.

Nancy frowned. "I almost wish I'd never found Carmen. Then I wouldn't feel so bad."

"If *you* feel bad," Mr. Drew said, "think of how Katie must feel right now."

"You're right, Daddy," Nancy said.

"Now," Mr. Drew said. He sat down next to Nancy with his own plate. "Are there any more questions before I dig in?"

"Yes!" Nancy said quickly.

"What?" Mr. Drew asked.

Nancy grinned. "Can you pass the ketchup? Please?"

Nancy went to bed early that night, but she couldn't sleep. As she tossed and turned, all she could think about was Katie and her secret. She finally fell asleep while counting parrots instead of sheep.

*　　　*　　　*

After breakfast the next morning, Hannah drove Nancy to Park Pals.

When Nancy walked into the clubhouse she saw Ranger Roy talking to Lynn. She also saw Todd standing next to Bess and George.

"Hi," Nancy said.

Todd folded his arms. "So, Detective Drew. Have you found Carmen yet?"

Nancy, Bess, and George looked at one another. They didn't say a word.

"Ha!" Todd laughed. "You *didn't* find Carmen. Some detective you are."

Bess stepped up to Todd. She pushed her face into his.

"For your information," Bess said, "Nancy *did* find Carmen."

Nancy clapped her hand over Bess's mouth. "Bess!"

But it was too late. Joey and Andrea were staring at her. Lynn and Ranger Roy were staring at her, too.

"Nancy?" Lynn asked. "Is Bess right? Did you find Carmen?"

Nancy took her hand off Bess's mouth. But her own mouth felt as dry as cotton.

"I—I—" Nancy stammered.

"Nancy, if you know where Carmen is, you must tell us," Ranger Roy said.

Nancy felt a big lump in her throat. She didn't have a choice anymore. She would have to tell Ranger Roy about Katie.

"I do know where Carmen is," Nancy said slowly. "Carmen is with—"

"Me," a voice said.

Nancy whirled around. Katie stood at the door with Lester's cage in her hand. Inside the cage was Carmen.

"Carmen is with me," Katie said.

"What?" Todd cried.

The Grasshoppers and the rangers surrounded Katie. She told them all about finding Carmen and wanting to keep her.

"Nancy, Bess, and George told me that keeping Carmen was wrong," Katie said. "It took me a while to realize they were right."

"They sure were," Ranger Roy said. He

gave the girls a big grin. "That's why I'm making all three of you Junior Park Rangers!"

"Yahoo!" Nancy shouted.

"That stinks!" Todd shouted.

When the girls were finished jumping up and down, Nancy went over to Ranger Roy.

"Katie brought Carmen back," she said. "Can she be a Junior Park Ranger, too?"

Ranger Roy took off his hat and scratched his head. Then he smiled.

"The more the merrier," he said.

Todd threw his own hat on the floor.

"Bummer!" he cried. "Now I'll never be a Junior Park Ranger. All I'll ever have is my stupid bug collection."

"Lynn told me about your bug collection," Ranger Roy said. "But I never had the pleasure of seeing it."

Bess jumped back as Todd pulled out his bug jar. He handed it to Ranger Roy.

Ranger Roy squinted as he examined the insects. "Is that a rove beetle I see?"

Todd nodded. "I found it under a rock."

Ranger Roy handed the jar back to Todd. "I can't make you a Junior Park Ranger, but I can give you a special summer job."

"A job?" Todd asked. "Doing what?"

"Working with the insects," Ranger Roy said. "Would you like that?"

"Would I!" Todd cried happily.

George leaned over to Nancy.

"Todd is finally going where he belongs," she whispered. "The bughouse."

Joey raised his hand. "How do we know this bird is really Carmen?" he asked.

The bright blue parrot stretched her neck. Then she began to sing.

"I'm a happy camper. That's what I like to do. I hope that you will join me, and be a camper tooooo. *Arrrrk!*"

"Does that answer your question?" Lynn said, laughing.

While the rangers and Grasshoppers gathered around the cage, Nancy sat down at the table. She opened her blue detective notebook and began to write:

* * *

I guess we're all happy campers now. And I was right. The most important thing was bringing Carmen home.

I think I'm going to like being a Junior Park Ranger. But probably not as much as I like being a detective!

Case closed.

The Hardy Boys® are:

THE CLUES BROTHERS™

By Franklin W. Dixon

Look for a brand-new story every other month

A MINSTREL® BOOK

Published by Pocket Books

1398-08

**Do your younger brothers and sisters
want to read books like yours?**

Let them know there are books just for them!

THE
NANCY DREW
NOTEBOOKS®

Look for a brand-new story every other month

Available from Minstrel® Books
Published by Pocket Books

1356-09

Sabrina The Teenage Witch™

Salem's Tails™

What's it like to be a powerful warlock,
sentenced to one hundred years in a
cat's body for trying to take over the world?

Ask Salem.

**Read all about Salem's magical
adventures in this new series based on the
hit ABC-TV show!**

#1 CAT TV
#2 Teacher's Pet
#3 You're History
#4 The King of Cats
#5 Dog day Afternoon
Salem Goes to Rome

Now available!
Look for a new title every other month

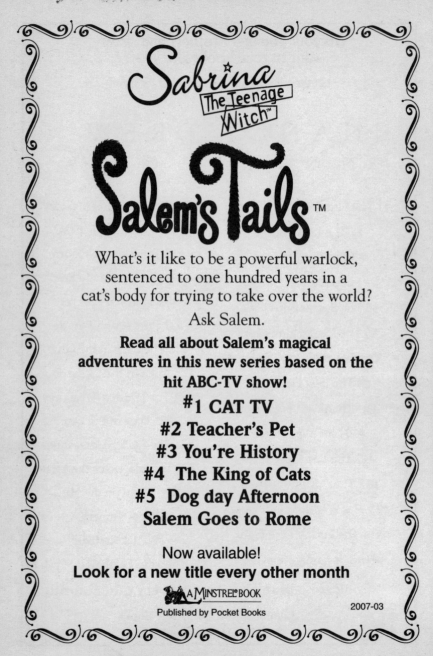

A MINSTREL® BOOK

Published by Pocket Books

2007-03